# Mail Order Bride Bryony's Destiny

### Faith Creek Brides
### Book 1

# Karla Gracey

Copyright © 2017 by Karla Gracey

All Rights Reserved. No part of this publication may be copied, reproduced in any format, by any means, electronic or otherwise, without prior consent from the copyright owner and publisher of this book.

This is a work of fiction. All characters, names, places and events are the product of the author's imagination or used fictitiously.

First Printing, 2017

## Dedication

I dedicate this book to my mother, as she was the one who kept urging me to write, and without her enthusiasm I would never written and published my books.

# Contents

| | |
|---|---|
| Chapter One ................................ 1 | Chapter Five ................................ 33 |
| Chapter Two ................................ 9 | Epilogue ....................................... 42 |
| Chapter Three ............................ 18 | Other books by Karla ................. 47 |
| Chapter Four .............................. 28 | About Karla Gracey ................... 48 |

# Chapter One

"I shan't," Edwin said, looking up at Bryony stubbornly. She sighed, and bent down to tie her charge's laces for him. He glowered down at her, his arms crossed as he fidgeted his feet every time she tried to grab a firm hold.

"Edwin, I know you miss your Mama and Papa, but making both our lives more difficult will not bring them home any more quickly," she said looking up at him, praying that for once he would accept that he couldn't win his own way. "I cannot bring them home. Nor can Mr Bailey, or Mrs Dalton." He winced a little as she spoke of the elderly butler and the kindly housekeeper. "Yes, I know you have been a menace for them too – and if I ever hear of you spilling the ashes from the nursery fire all over the front parlor, or anything equally ill-natured again I shall have to inform your parents and I doubt they will be pleased." Edwin did at least have the decency to look chagrined, but he was clearly still determined not to cooperate. "You cannot keep making work for everyone else. They have enough to do," Bryony said getting to her feet. "Now, if you will not put on your boots and your coat and assist me with the shopping, then I shall go to the park alone today and I shall cancel your birthday party tomorrow too."

"You wouldn't," he exclaimed, his face quickly changing to a look of horror.

"Oh, but I would. A big boy like you, only a day from your tenth birthday, is more than capable of tying his own laces, and of understanding that his actions have consequences." She turned, pulled on her own hat and coat and made to leave the house. Edwin grabbed her hand. She turned round, and tried her best to keep a stern look upon her face.

"I'll be good," he whispered and bent down, fumbling with his boots. She watched as he carefully pulled his boots tight and then tied the laces in a neat bow. Deep in concentration, his little tongue poked out of the side of his mouth. She wanted to smile, but knew she could not. He stood back up, his little back straight as he awaited her appraisal.

"See," she said. "You can do it. And before we go you will apologize to Mrs Dalton, and to Alice who had to clean up the mess you left behind". Bryony kept her tone firm. He nodded. Bryony was new to being a nanny. She usually worked in the kitchens, assisting Mrs Wilson who was the finest cook in Baltimore, but the unexpected departure of Nanny Purvis, just a day after Mr and Mrs Haverthwaite had left to go to New York for a month, had meant she had been forced to step into a role she was ill equipped and utterly inexperienced to undertake. She was more used to indulging young Edwin than punishing him and holding him to account, and it was taking every effort to maintain a firm hand.

"But…" he tailed off, looking sheepish.

"No buts, run along now and find them." She sighed with relief as he rushed towards the back stairs. Maybe there was hope for him yet – and for her too. She followed him at a more sedate pace, and was heartened to see him give Mrs Dalton and Alice a genuine apology. He could be a menace, but he had a generous spirit. He was simply lonely, and did not understand why his parents continually disappeared from his life. If only they could find a nanny for him that would be consistent, would give him the stability they could not. But he had already had four different guardians this year, and it was still only May.

"Well done," she said as he ran to her side, his face beaming with pride. "But, you must remember to mean what you say, an apology is no good unless you do your very best to make sure you never do such a thing again."

"I know Bry'ny. Sorry - Miss Shaw," he corrected himself. It must be so confusing for him, that one day she was just Bryony the kitchen girl, and then the next she was his nanny and guardian. She put her arm around his shoulder and guided him back upstairs, and out of the door.

The streets were busy, and usually Edwin would be rushing about – his curiosity getting him into everything – but today he stayed close to her side as they went about their errands. She assumed he was doing his very best to appear contrite, that he meant to mend his ways. She was glad of the calm. They made a quick stop at the bakery to order a fine birthday cake, a more lengthy one at the postal office to collect a parcel and mail some letters, and a final visit to Mr MacGregor's hardware store to pick up a new broom handle for Alice. Edwin did not leave her side for a moment, not even to look at the fancy cakes and fairings. Bryony was proud of him for being so responsible. "So, are you ready to go to the park now?" she asked him brightly, as he took the broom handle for her.

"I don't think I want to," he said quietly. It was not like him to be so docile, and she couldn't help but feel a little concerned. She knelt down and looked him in the eye. His face had gone quite pale. She put her hand to his forehead, he was burning up.

"Does anything hurt?" she asked him. He shook his head.

"No, I just don't feel like going to the park," he said bravely.

"Edwin, we don't have to go to the park. We don't have to do anything at all – in truth I think it might be best if you got some rest. You have a fever, and I think I should get you home straight away, but usually when people are unwell there is something particular that hurts. You aren't being any trouble if you are unwell."

"I just feel peculiar..." He didn't finish his sentence, his eyes closed and his skin went ashen. His little body swayed and would have hit the sidewalk if Bryony hadn't caught him. She caught him up in her arms, and leaving the parcel and the broom handle where they lay she rushed him back to the house.

Mr Bailey opened the door, his usual sneer in place ready to greet whoever had deigned to ring the bell, but when he saw Bryony with Edwin shivering in her arms he blanched. "I shall send for the doctor," he said, his eyes showing his concern and affection for the usually boisterous little boy. Bryony rushed past him and up the stairs to the boy's room. She laid him down on the bed, and quickly stripped him out of his boots and clothes. She pulled a clean nightgown over his head and put him into bed. She tucked the coverlet around him snugly and went in search of more blankets. She bundled him up, and felt his cheeks and his forehead. His face was slick with sweat, and yet his body was reacting as if it was ice cold, his teeth chattering and his tiny body shivering so violently he looked possessed.

Bryony raced to the washstand, taking a soft cloth from the shelf she poured water into the bowl and took it to his side. She began to bathe his head, down his arms and his hands. He shuddered as she held the cloth at the back of his neck. She could feel tears pouring down her cheeks as she sat, helpless, at his side. She prayed that the doctor would come quickly, that there would be something that could be done. Edwin was a sweet boy, a little mischievous of course, but he only did what he did because he craved attention in a house full of servants who were too busy to play with him.

She sat up suddenly. How would she ever be able to tell his parents? How would she get word to them quickly, that they needed to come, to be here by their son's side? She stood and paced up and down, knowing it was unlikely that her employers had even received Mr Bailey's letter telling them that Nanny Purvis had left the household – how could she now say that not only had their son been deserted, with nobody but the servants, and that he was so very sick.

"How can I help?" Mrs Dalton asked, entering the room. Bryony looked at her, barely knowing what to say.

"I, I don't know," she stuttered. "I just don't know."

"Mr Bailey has sent for the doctor, he will be here shortly. What do you think it might be?"

"I don't know. It was so sudden. One minute he seemed quite well – as you know when we left here. But he was quiet and didn't leave my side whilst we carried out our errands, and then he was so pale and so hot," she said, knowing her voice sounded panicked. "His parents should know, but how on earth do we tell them this?"

"Children get fevers," Mrs Dalton said confidently. "They usually recover from them very swiftly. It might be worth us waiting until the doctor has been before we concern them."

"What if the doctor cannot help? What if Edwin doesn't recover quickly?" Bryony asked anxiously. Mrs Dalton sighed heavily.

"I don't know, but once we know more I will see if I can send a telegraph to the Haverthwaite's hotel. The office may be closed by the time I get there, but I will try."

"Even if it is not serious, he needs his parents. He is scared and alone, and they should care enough to be here for him," Bryony said a little bitterly. Mrs Dalton nodded her agreement, but said nothing, squeezing Bryony's arm as she left the room.

She sank back down onto the chair beside the bed, and continued to sponge the little boy's burning skin. "Edwin, you can fight this," she assured him, though all she could think of was watching another little boy, her youngest brother, as he fought a sickness that had come on just as suddenly, and had been just as inexplicable. But the Shaw's had lived in a filthy tenement, Edwin in this fine townhouse. Her family had fought for every scrap of food, and battled against leaking roofs and draughty windows to keep warm and dry. Edwin had never been cold or hungry in his life. He had to be stronger than Michael had been. He had to survive, as Michael had not. She knew she would be blamed if anything happened to him, and not only would she lose another little boy that she had come to love, but she would lose her position and be out on the streets with no character to recommend her. "You have to get well," she hissed against his forehead as she pressed a kiss to his fevered brow. "You have to."

"Miss Shaw, good day to you." Doctor Harris nodded at Bryony as he entered the room, took off his top hat and put it down on the dresser. He moved to the bed, and placed his large leather bag at Edwin's feet. He opened it and took out the instruments he required and began to examine the boy. Bryony stood, stalking her way around the bed like a protective tigress, concerned about her cub. She watched as the doctor listened to Edwin's breathing, noted the pallor of his skin, measured his temperature and marked it in his notes carefully. "Did he complain of any pain?"

"No, I thought he was just being brave but I think he was just feeling so awful that there wasn't anything specific. He hasn't once clutched at his belly, or his head. He just lies there, listless and sweating though he shivers as though he were in the depths of winter."

"It may be a number of things, but I think it is most likely to be influenza," Dr Harris said finally.

"He will get well?"

"I cannot tell, but he is a healthy and strong boy normally?" She nodded.

"A little too boisterous at times," she smiled weakly as she remembered that he had just that morning caused such havoc.

"Then there is a good chance he will be up and about in no time." Bryony noticed the look of doubt on his face, but she didn't say a word. He rummaged in his bag and pulled out a large bottle and a smaller vial. Carefully he poured some of the golden brown liquid from the larger vessel into the tiny bottle and handed it to her. "This is laudanum. Use it very sparingly, just to help him sleep. No more than 1 drop for a boy his size in a glass of water." She clasped the medicine in her hand. "I shall drop by tomorrow to check on him."

"Thank you doctor," she said and moved to see him out.

"No, you stay with our patient," he assured her. "He needs you more than I." She nodded and sank down into the chair by Edwin's side once more. She would not leave his side until he was well.

The day went by agonizingly slowly, and Bryony was exhausted by the time night fell. The clock struck seven. She stood and stretched. Mrs Dalton appeared in the doorway, a tray full of food in her hands. "I thought you might need some sustenance, and I brought some chicken broth for Edwin – maybe we might be able to get him to sip at it?" she said.

"I probably should eat something, though I have little appetite," Bryony admitted. "But Edwin will need his strength, so some of your broth may be just the thing."

"You go and have a rest for a few hours," the housekeeper said. "I can take care of him, feed him his supper. You will be no good to any of us if you are dead on your feet." Bryony wanted to take her up on the generous offer, but Edwin was her charge. She would not leave him. She shook her head. "At least go and sit in the corner and read the newspaper for a short while then, and eat your own supper?" Mrs Dalton said firmly.

Bryony watched as the plump housekeeper picked up the bowl of broth and perched on the edge of the bed. Slowly and tenderly she began to spoon it into Edwin's parched lips. Knowing she would not win an argument with the doughty older woman, she picked up her plate, piled high with bread and butter, cheese and ham, and took it and the newspaper to a chair by the window. She sat down, and with the very first bite realized just how hungry she was. She ravenously polished off the entire plate, and went and got herself a piece of seedcake from the tray. Once replete, she sat down and began to read the newspaper as she listened to Mrs Dalton crooning lullabies to Edwin.

There was little in the newspaper that brought her joy. The headline was all about an outbreak of influenza that had already claimed four lives. She prayed it would not take Edwin's – or anyone else in the Haverthwaite household's - life. Needing cheering she flicked to the matrimonial section. She thought it funny that men and women across the country might think that this was a suitable way to come together and make a successful marriage, but it seemed that many did. Some of the advertisements were so serious that they made her giggle, and she needed something to make her smile right now. She perused the desperate gentlemen of Dakota, and Montana – all in need of a docile bride who wanted little more out of life than to cook and clean and pick up after their man. She grinned at an advertisement that claimed its subscriber wanted a well-educated and ambitious wife. She had never yet met a man who truly wanted a wife with goals of her own, and she was sure that the gentleman in Wyoming might ultimately come to know that a little too late. But one of the advertisements kept drawing her eye back to it, again and again. Its absolute honesty was something she had never seen before, and she couldn't help but admire a man who had the courage to be so frank.

> *A gentleman of Texas seeks to correspond with a young woman with strength and determination with a view to marriage. A sunny disposition and a love of hard work for good reward is most essential, and an understanding that a ranching life may mean many lonely nights and challenging days. The subscriber enjoys music and literature, and it would be preferred if any applicants did too. It would be sheer bliss to have someone to share such pleasures, and life's tribulations with the right woman. All replies to box 383, The Baltimore Sun.*

## Chapter Two

A cheerful whistle always preceded Wilbur Marlow. Cody grinned as he heard the popular ditty his neighbor so loved coming closer. The cows moved gracefully aside, as though the sound had them mesmerized. "You the pied piper?" Cody teased as Wilbur appeared, sauntering slowly and contentedly through the herd.

"I would never lure children, or rats," Wilbur said with a grin. "No, my abilities are only with those of a bovine nature." They both laughed. "Your girls are looking well."

"They have come through calving well, and I shall be rewarded with plenty of milk."

"I saw you'd separated out the herd. So you have decided to become a dairy farmer then?" Wilbur asked. When he arrived in Texas Cody had not been sure whether he wished to become a rancher, or to keep his herd and provide milk, butter and cheese for the little town of Faith Creek. The land around the little town was little suited to farming, with its iron-rich red earth and dry climate, little grew without a lot of effort. Most of his neighbors were miners, trackers and traders. The lack of fresh food had meant that over the winter many families had struggled. It had made him think long and hard about what he could do to help. There was more money in ranching to be sure, but little satisfaction if his greed left his neighbors hungry. He had the opportunity to be able to provide them with good quality, filling food. If he did it right, any surplus could be sold at the bigger markets in Dallas and Houston. He could still make good money, but he could help care for his community too. Wilbur had been his confidant and a source of sound advice, over an ale in the saloon on many an occasion.

"It wasn't a hard decision in the end," Cody admitted. ""This way I get enough meat to support my own needs, maybe even sell a little from the steers, but I get a reliable and steady income from the dairy – whilst providing local people with good food that fills their bellies and does them good. I've been up since the crack of dawn separating the calves from their mothers so I can get started. I would have spoken with you about it before, but you haven't been around. Where've you been since January my friend?"

"I went a wanderin'," Wilbur said with a smile. "Been staying with my daughter and her new husband in Fort Worth. I'm a Grandpappy now." He looked so proud he might burst his buttons. Cody was happy for him.

"Eleanor is well?"

"She is, and my grandbaby is so purty, she'll break some hearts when she is grown – I do not doubt it."

"I am glad to hear it."

"She asked after you," Wilbur said slyly. "Wondered if you've found yourself a good wife yet."

"I hope you told her that it is none of her business, as she left me high and dry at the altar all those years ago," Cody said dryly, though he held no malice towards his former love. He and Eleanor had grown up together, back in Fort Worth. Always inseparable from the earliest age, she was married to another man now, and happier than he could ever have made her.

"Aw, she didn't mean nothin' by it. She still loves you, wants you to be happy," Wilbur said, patting his large belly. He noticed a small stain, and began to pick at it. "Egg custard," he stated with certainty.

"She still makes those pastries then?"

"She does, and that husband o' hers thinks they should set up a bakery. Thinks they could make their fortunes."

"He may just about be right. I've never known anyone able to bake a pie like Eleanor. I'd pay a good price, and I'm sure others will too. She'll be the most popular baker in town," Cody admitted fairly, but wished they might change the subject of the conversation.

"Now, rumor has it you are in need of some help here," Wilbur said doing just that, his face serious for a change. Cody sighed, glad for the shift. He didn't need Eleanor's big brown eyes and perfect cooking to be drifting around his head too much. It would only make him feel more lonely than he already did.

"Now who told you that?" Cody asked. He had been complaining in the saloon that he had too much to do, but everyone in town did that. Texas was not the easiest place to settle and make your way, and though he had been born and raised in the State, it had taken a lot of courage to make the move to Faith Creek, to start his own herd without his banker father's money behind him. Every man in town knew that he was the master of his own destiny, that it was down to him to make the land pay – whatever way he could, and Cody was no exception. Maybe his desire to prove himself was even greater than most. He'd come out here with soft hands and a soft brain according to his father. He looked down at his hands now. They were stained with dirt, callused and tanned nut brown. He couldn't tell if his brain had done any hardening – but they sure had.

"Young Barlow said might have mentioned you were a little browbeaten," Wilbur said with a wink. "Thinks that you've bitten off more than you can chew and is prayin' you fail so'n he can buy your land when you give up."

"He may be right about having too much to do, but he clearly doesn't know me at all if he thinks I would ever sell to him. I'll not give over good land and healthy animals to a man like him who will break both in a month to pay for his gambling." Cody could feel the anger inside him welling up. His father had been just as dismissive when he had announced his intention to come to Faith Creek to make his own fortune, and he was determined to prove both men wrong.

"Well, I find myself at a loose end. I have people who do all my work for me these days, and I'm bored," Wilbur admitted. He had come here to Faith Creek when it was little more than a trading post, right up by the New Mexico border, to find gold when Cody and Eleanor had been just children, and unlike the many who failed, Wilbur had found just what he came looking for. A rich seam, that became a prosperous mine, had given him enough money to do whatever he pleased until the day he died.

"You don't intend going back to Fort Worth to be with Eleanor and the baby then?" Cody asked, surprised.

"Hell no," Wilbur exploded. "Sure it was nice visitin', but I'd forgot how much I hate that town. All those people and the smell!" Cody chuckled. He felt the same way about the place he had grown up in. He loved the wide open spaces here, and the fresh air and the honesty and simplicity of the men and women who lived and worked all the hours God sent to scratch a living. Having grown up the son of a wealthy banker it had been more than refreshing to be amongst people who spoke their mind and weren't afraid of a hard day's work. "No, you're stuck with me here in Faith Creek," Wilbur said solemnly. "This place has gotten into my bones, and I intend to live here and die here. Now, do you want some help, or shall I take my sorry self down into town and find someone else who needs a hard workin' man?"

Wilbur had always been the father Cody had wished he had. He had been looking forward to being able to call the eccentric old coot his father-in-law. But that eventuality had never come about. Eleanor was happy, she had everything she had ever wanted and he was glad for her – but it didn't stop him missing her from time to time. He had chosen Faith Creek because of Wilbur. His friendship and support of Cody's dream had given him the strength to see it through. To have him working alongside him would be more than he could have ever hoped for. "How are you at milking cows?" he joked.

"I'm adequate, but I don't like it," he joked.

"Then what use are you to me?" Cody asked laughing with the older man.

"Well, as a boy I used to make the best cheese in New York State, before my Daddy brought us all here to Texas." Cody stared at him. This was a part of the old boy's story he had never heard. He couldn't help but be intrigued about what else he did not know, but now was not the time to ask.

"You know your way around a dairy?"

"I do, I can make you the finest butter and cheese, skim your cream and take care of all that milk. I won't lie, I don't really want to work with your girls here. They're a bit smelly and dirty for me these days. I like to keep my suits nice," he said grinning from ear to ear.

"You wouldn't even come and whistle to them while I milk them? It keeps them so calm, I can't help but think it might make everything much easier."

"Oh, I might just manage that for you my boy," Wilbur said happily. Cody felt a weight lift from his shoulders. Maybe this crazy plan of his might just work after all. He had known it would be nigh on impossible alone, but with Wilbur by his side he was sure that he could make it pay, and then he just might be able to bring home a bride and have a family of his own. He was tired of being lonely, and he needed help and support from somewhere.

He led Wilbur from the field, closed the gate carefully and took him to see the dairy. Wilbur seemed impressed by the clean, tiled room with the large vats ready to make cheese and the churns for the butter. Rows of large, lidded pails were lined up against the wall ready to be filled with the rich, fresh milk, and he had crates of bottles ready for the thick, yellowy cream. Wilbur let out a wolf whistle. "Well my boy, if you are sure you trust me, I think I could be very happy in here," he said.

"I trust you," Cody said. "I am glad this will be your domain, it has had me almost scared to death. I'd bought a couple of books, and was going to hope I could learn what I needed to from there."

"Nothing to fear, I'll teach you everything you need to know – and those books may just help us do it even better than I can already."

"I am more than eager to learn, but not today. I've got work to do with the cows. I'll get them milked, and then you can get going." Wilbur rubbed his hands gleefully, and started to get together some cleaning implements.

"I'll wash down," he said. Cody turned and walked towards the door. "Oh, and I left a pile of letters up at the house for you. John Kimball gave me 'em. Said they came from out East." His eyes were curious, but Cody ignored the unasked questions. He wasn't ready to talk about his little plan to find himself a wife just yet, not until he was sure he had found himself a woman he felt was right for him and the life here.

He walked back to the herd, and carefully began to move them through the series of gates into the milking shed. He kept glancing back at the house, wondering what those letters might contain. But he had work to do. He needed to make the farm prosperous before he brought a wife here, and so he had to put the work first. Wilbur needed to be able to get the cheese maturing, and they needed to get out to the markets and talk to the grocers and general store owners to get their milk on the shelves in every store from Lubbock to Amarillo.

With his girls in their stalls, contentedly munching on hay, he started milking. It was hard work, on the hands and the back especially, and it took a lot of time. Cody wondered if he might be able to hire a couple of young lads to assist him, or even lasses. Times were tough and many families could use the extra money. But he didn't have cash to pay them. He wondered if anyone would be prepared to help out, if he promised them a gallon of milk, a quart of cream or a pound of butter. It wouldn't hurt asking around, though he doubted he would get much interest. Most people roundabouts were busy, making their own land pay.

Finally each cow was back in the field. He made his way through to the dairy, where he found Wilbur carefully adding something to a large vat of the milk, stirring it through carefully. "This will make the curds and whey separate out," he said. "Then the magic begins. But that'll take time. I've churned your first butter, and the pails are filled and ready to be delivered into town."

"You don't hang around do you my friend?" Cody said. Wilbur slapped him on the back.

"Get the cart, and I'll take everything down with me when I go." Cody loaded up the wagon, and smiled as Wilbur set off along the track into Faith Creek. He wondered how well the fresh milk would sell. Well, he would soon find out if his gamble had been worth taking.

Tired and happy he sank into the pine chair he kept out on the porch. Wilbur had left the letters on the table there, and he picked them up and began to sort through them. He could tell nothing from the envelopes. The handwriting on each one was the same, and the return address was for the newspaper. He ripped the first one open, and a second envelope fell out. He picked it up. The paper was thin, and he could almost read the letter inside through it. He opened it cautiously, not wanting to tear the flimsy missive inside. He sighed, the woman was in her forties and had three children. He was not ready to take on a ready-made family – and he would prefer his bride to be closer to his own age. The next applicant was just eighteen, he dismissed her just as swiftly. He didn't want an angry child, running away from her parents. He needed a partner and helpmeet.

None of the women seemed right, and the pile of rejected applicants grew quickly. He was left with just three letters. He decided he needed a drink before he read them, so went inside and put the kettle on the stove. He made himself a strong coffee, and added a dash of cream from his own herd, and a splash of whiskey to fortify himself. He took it back outside, with a plate of almost stale bread and a slab of boiled bacon. He set them down on the table, and picked up the letter on top of the now tiny pile of unread responses. He settled into the chair, and began to read.

*Dear Gentleman Of Texas,*

*Can I commend you on the first, and probably only, genuinely truthful advertisement I have ever seen in the*

Matrimonials section? I was genuinely impressed that you were so candid. So much so, that rather than scorning your advertisement as I usually do with such things I found myself prompted to reply. Something I have never even considered before.

  My name is Bryony Shaw. My mother was Irish, my father Scots and they came here to Baltimore when they wed to try and make a better life for themselves. From all their tales life back in their homelands was very hard, but so was settling here in America. We lived in the tenements in New York, near the docks, when I was a girl. But we moved here to Baltimore after they lost my younger brother. He had cholera. I don't think they ever got over it really. Sadly they both passed away last year. Papa in an accident at work, and I think Mama pined so for him and my baby brother that her heart finally gave up.

  I work in service. I am a kitchen maid in a big house, and am second to the Cook, Mrs Wilson. She is the finest cook in the city, or so everyone says. I have learned much from her. Our employers are rarely home, but they have a young son who I am temporarily acting as a Nanny to. Sadly he is very unwell, and it is bringing back so many memories of losing Michael, my brother, so I am terribly sorry if this letter seems maudlin. I am generally of quite a sunny disposition, but I am most concerned for poor Edwin. I just hope he has the strength to fight what the doctor has said is Influenza.

  As to your criteria, I am hardworking and used to long days and often waking nights too. I have only ever lived in town, but I am strong and I learn quickly. I am a good cook, as you might expect from my employment, but I am also good with animals and children.

  I would so very much like to know more about you, and do sincerely hope that this letter finds you well. Please tell me all about yourself, your family and your life in Texas. I am most intrigued.

  Yours, Most Sincerely

  Bryony Shaw

Cody smiled. Bryony Shaw was frank and honest. She wrote of things that many people might keep bottled up inside and never speak of – to a complete stranger. He wondered if she was as forthright in person, and whether she would fit in, here in Faith Creek. He couldn't help but think that she would. She struck him as the kind of woman who would brook no nonsense, and she had clearly survived much hardship and was still fighting. Yes, it was safe to say that he liked Bryony Shaw.

# Chapter Three

Dear Miss Shaw,

    I cannot tell you how delighted I was to receive your letter. You are a true breath of fresh air. Please, do be assured I did not think you maudlin at all. You wrote of your concerns and your cares, and I would hope that you will continue to tell me of them for many years to come. I like that you show such compassion, such feeling for those in your family and the household you work in. I do hope that your young charge is much recovered by the time you receive this letter.

    I am a dairy farmer. I had considered ranching, but Faith Creek had a hard winter and it got me thinking that there were things I could have done to help my neighbors and friends, had I had food to offer them when things were at their worst. Of course, I could probably make more money ranching, but Texas has enough wealthy cattlemen. We need more people producing food and jobs for local people – not make more money for those wealthy enough to put beef on their tables every day of the year. There is a long way to go before the dairy will be profitable, and it will mean a lot of long days and nights ahead. I do not doubt that there will be hardship at times, and I am in no way a wealthy man with anything to fall back upon should all of this go wrong.

My family are all still living. My parents live in Fort Worth, near Dallas where my father owns a bank. But do not be fooled by that, my Papa disowned me when I refused to go to college and follow in his footsteps. Mama keeps telling me he will get over it in her letters, but there is no sign of it at present. I have a sister, who married well and has produced perfect grandchildren for my father to be proud of. I believe I am a disappointment to him in that respect too! I do not doubt that I have been written out of Papa's will and my nephews will have been included in my stead. I do not mind, truthfully. I often think my Papa is burdened by his wealth, rather than blessed by it. He has no clue what to do with money, other than to hoard it and keep it safe. I am no spendthrift, but I doubt I could allow myself to sit on such sums knowing there are hungry, sick and troubled people in the world who needed it more.

Dear Miss Shaw, Bryony, would you like to come and visit? I know we barely know one another, and such an idea is somewhat foolhardy – reckless even. I had intended for us to have a long, and respectable courtship, and I know many might think me too forward. But I feel like I have known you for a lifetime, I have rarely felt able to be so open with anyone other than my dear friend Wilbur. He runs my dairy, and I would be lost without him. But if you would like to meet, I can come to Baltimore, or you can use the tickets I have enclosed with this letter to come to Texas. Faith Creek is a small place, tucked up against the New Mexico border, but it has its charms. The people are friendly, and if I were to meet the train in Fort Worth I can take you to the finest little bakery in the entire United States.

I do so hope you will come, and I will be forever glad that you chose to respond to my advertisement. I cannot promise you an *easy life, and it will certainly be one full of toil – but I can assure you that I would always take care of you to the best of my ability.*

*Yours most truly*

*Cody Jenkins*

Bryony clutched the letter to her breast and tried to keep the smile from her face. He truly seemed to like her, was eager that they should meet. She had not expected him to even respond, had been so sure that there would have been prettier, though he could no nothing of any of the respondents looks from a letter of course, and more suitable candidates that would have replied to him. Yet, he had chosen her. He appeared to be kind and generous. His enquiry after Edwin's health touched her. Thankfully the lad was quite recovered, thought it had been a very difficult few weeks as they waited for the fever to fully subside.

"Bryony, could you come down please?" Mrs Haverthwaite called up the back stair well, to where the servants had their rooms. Bryony quickly pulled on a clean apron, smoothed it down and rushed down the stairs.

"Yes Ma'am," she said politely.

"Come through into the parlor dear, I would like to speak with you for a moment." Bryony followed the elegantly dressed woman, always staying a few steps behind. She wondered how Alice managed to make their mistress' blonde locks curl in such elegant ways, and how the pins stayed in all day. Bryony hair was thick, and a dark rich brown that seemed to have a life of its own. She seemed to have to re-pin it almost every hour, it was so unruly.

"Please take a seat," Mrs Haverthwaite indicated one of the comfortable chairs by the fire as they entered the sunny, south facing room. They were upholstered in a pretty floral fabric that reminded Bryony of her mother's Sunday best dress. She sat, perching on the very edge of the chair, not daring to relax. "Do not look so concerned," the lady of the house said with a smile. "I simply wished to thank you for everything you did for Edwin after that dreadful Nanny left us all in the lurch like that."

"It was nothing, Ma'am," Bryony said, as Mrs Haverthwaite

moved to a silver tea service laid out on the table.

"Would you like some tea?" Bryony nodded, though she would really rather be sent back to the kitchen where she belonged. "Do you take milk?"

"I do, and one sugar if I may please," she responded politely. Mrs Haverthwaite brought her a delicate bone china cup and saucer, and a matching side plate with a piece of fruit cake upon it. Bryony watched her pour her own beverage, and waited anxiously to see how her mistress would eat the cake with the tiny fork and spoon she had laid daintily on the side of each of their plates. Mrs Haverthwaite put her cup and saucer down on the occasional table by her side, and using her fork and spoon like a knife and fork cut a dainty portion and popped it elegantly into her mouth. Bryony did her best to copy her, but it was clearly an art that took years of training to do so skillfully. Eventually she decided to put the cake down, and sip at the tea. That was at least something she was familiar with.

"Bryony," Mrs Haverthwaite began softly.

"Yes Ma'am."

"I want to thank you for your care of Edwin, and for contacting us so promptly when he fell sick. We had only received the letter about Nanny Purvis the day your telegram came, so it was all quite a shock. To come home and see the poor boy so unwell was a horror. But watching you with him, I cannot think of anyone better to take care of him. Would you consider being his Nanny? Of course it would mean a rise in your wages, and you would be entitled to the large room beside the nursery."

"Mrs Haverthwaite, I am not qualified to be a Nanny. I can teach Edwin little but how to bake an excellent sponge and to make a short pastry," she said, stunned.

"I can hire him a tutor to teach him anything he needs to know before he leaves for school when he turns eleven, but it is a gentle hand and someone to care for him he needs most."

Bryony bit at the inside of her cheek, as she thought about what Edwin really needed. She wanted to remind his mother that all he really desired was to have his parents notice him, to be there for him. But it was not her place. They truly were offering her an incredible opportunity, and many girls in service would already have been saying thank you, and that they would not let their employers down. But since she had responded to Mr Jenkins's advertisement, something had come over her. She was developing a disregard for keeping her place, for toeing the line and doing as she was told. A little devil inside her kept insisting that there was something so much better waiting for her somewhere; maybe it was in Texas on a dairy farm with a man who appreciated her honesty?

"Mrs Haverthwaite," she started, a little cautiously. She had never spoken back to anyone before. "Though I am highly flattered by your faith in my abilities, and though I can categorically state that I do care for Edwin most deeply, I cannot accept your offer. Edwin does not need another Nanny before he goes to school. What he needs is to know that his parents love him, that they want to spend time with him and wish to teach him about their world themselves. It can be counted on two hands the amount of days you have spent here in Baltimore with him in the past seven months, and he misses you terribly, every time you leave. When you come home he is so excited. He can hardly contain himself. He flourishes in the glow of your presence, but when you leave him again he becomes morose and difficult. It can take us weeks to bring him back out of his shell. He acts out, and drives his Nanny, and all of the staff half mad with his antics. He becomes the good, kind and gentle boy you see for such a brief time – usually just as you return home and it starts all over again." Bryony had spoken her words quickly, and she could see her employer's face reddening with every word she spoke, but she no longer cared for her own position. She cared that Edwin would get the family he so desperately needed.

"Miss Shaw, I think it best if you pack your things and leave this house immediately," Mrs Haverthwaite said through tightly pursed lips. "How dare you speak to me in such a way? You are nothing but a kitchen maid. What do you know of bringing up a young gentleman?"

"Clearly more than you do, as you left me to do your job for you," Bryony retorted. "When you act as a loving parent does, fighting tooth and nail for your child then maybe I might believe you have the right to condemn me for caring how Edwin is treated. I do not ask you to listen to me because I am right. I ask you to listen to Edwin. I am glad to go. I cannot sit by any longer and watch that poor boy being denied the love his parents should be giving him because they are too busy and wrapped up in their own affairs to even notice him. If you did not want the responsibility of a child, maybe you should not have had one," she finished rudely. Mrs Haverthwaite's face was a picture of outrage, and Bryony almost giggled to see her so put out. But she did not regret a single word she had said.

"You shall leave here without a character," the older woman fumed. "You will never find work in a respectable household in Baltimore again – I shall see to it."

"I do not need your silly character. I do not need Baltimore," Bryony said with a grin. "There is a big, wide world outside that door – as you well know, you have travelled to so many countries and cities, leaving behind your poor son to pine for you. I shall survive without your approval."

"How can you be so foolish, so selfish, so reckless?" Mrs Haverthwaite spluttered.

"I shall go upstairs and pack Ma'am," Bryony said deferentially. "If you could ensure my wages are ready for me upon my return. I shall leave immediately. I have a train to catch."

"A train to catch?" Edwin's face was ashen as he peered around the door. "You are leaving me Bry'ny?" Her heart sank. She had not meant for him to overhear their conversation. In truth she had not expected to say any of the terribly hurtful, though painfully true, things that she had just thrown at Mrs Haverthwaite. But she would never have wanted Edwin to think she did not care for him, or to overhear her saying that she was sure his own mother did not love him.

"Oh, Edwin," she said rushing to kneel by his side. "I wanted to tell you myself, not like this. I hadn't intended to go quite so soon, but I am going to Texas to be married," she tried to make her voice sound light, as though she were giving him the most wonderful news in the world.

"Mama, are you really going to send me away to school soon?" he asked, turning to his mother, his little fists balled tightly.

"Oh Edwin, do not be silly child. Every little boy must go to school. Your father went to the very same school we have in mind for you. He had a wonderful time there, made such wonderful friends. You will have the time of your life," Mrs Haverthwaite said defensively.

"So what Bry'ny - sorry Miss Shaw said is true?" he asked. His mother looked perplexed. "You don't want me? You don't love me?" he asked bravely, a solitary tear falling down his chubby cheek.

"Of course I care for you Edwin. I am your mother, and your father does too," Mrs Haverthwaite said defensively, but there was no warmth in her voice, and her glare was flinty. "But he is a busy man and I must accompany him when he travels for his work."

"Why can you not take me with you?"

"Oh Edwin, your father is a politician. It is simply not easy for us to take you with us, to have you with us at all times - though of course we would wish to."

"I do not believe you. Why do you not love me? Why does Papa not ever want me to be around?" he asked, with the clarity and directness only a child can have. Bryony wished that none of this had happened, that he had never heard them. She wanted to scoop him up into her arms and reassure him that everything would be alright. That his Mama and Papa did love him, truly - but that they just weren't very good at showing it. But she did not. She watched as his Mother failed to find an answer, as she stuttered and stammered, trying to placate him - but unable to find the three simple words he needed to hear the most.

"Bryony, can I come with you?" the boy asked simply, turning away from his mother to face her. His little face was so earnest, his eyes so sad. She longed to say yes.

"Edwin, you know you cannot," she said, brushing his dark curls back off his face and cupping his cheek. "You belong with your family."

"You do not want me either?" he said, hurt.

"No, that is not true. I would take you with me in a heartbeat - but you are a Haverthwaite, and your Mama and Papa would miss you terribly.

Tears began to pour down her own cheeks, but Mrs Haverthwaite looked as though she had been turned to stone.

"Take the boy," she said spitefully. "How could I ever love him anyway?" Bryony looked at her questioningly, but it seemed that the older woman was not looking at her and Edwin any more. She stared past them. Bryony turned to see Mr Haverthwaite standing in the doorway. His face was puce with rage.

"Muriel, you promised never to speak of this," he said, his voice icy cold. She nodded nervously.

"I am sorry William, I never meant to say a word. You know I did not," she said, her voice and gestures that of a supplicant trying to regain his favor.

"But you did. You made me a promise and you have broken it. But there is little to be done now. You," he said turning his angry gaze upon Bryony. "If you want him, take him. I shall see you get an allowance for his support."

"I'm sorry Sir, Ma'am?" she queried, unfazed by the tension and anger in the room. Her only concern was the boy, standing by her side quaking with emotions he could not control. "Should we not speak of this when the boy is not present?" Neither of them answered her. They continued to glower at one another. She bent down and kissed Edwin on the cheek. "Go upstairs to your room. Do not stay and eavesdrop. I shall come upstairs to you as soon as I can," she assured him. He shook his head firmly.

"No Bryony, I think I should know, don't you – why they don't want me, why they have never wanted me?" She nodded, his point was more than valid. She stood upright, putting her hands on his shoulders. He was such a brave little soul, and he had such a loving heart. She would fight for him, because he needed her to. She would gladly fight for him for the rest of her life if it was required. She turned back to her employers.

"So, do I understand that you want me to take your son with me when I leave?"

"He is not my son," Mrs Haverthwaite spat. "How could I ever love her brat?"

"I will not have you speak of Emmeline that way," Mr Haverthwaite said.

"Why ever shouldn't I? She was after all your harlot was she not?"

"No, she was not. She was my brother's daughter, and she came to me when she needed help."

"Your brother was unmarried and had no children," Mrs Haverthwaite said dismissively, as if the facts were irrelevant. Bryony felt sure that she had convinced herself of a truth, and no matter what Mr Haverthwaite said it would be of no consequence to the older woman's beliefs. She saw herself as the victim, the woman forced to bring up a child not her own because of her husband's infidelities, and she would cling to her sense of outrage as it was all she had left.

"Not entirely true my dear, Bennett has a number of illegitimate children – why do you think I refuse to see him when he has left so many women in such straits without a care for their welfare? Emmeline was destitute, and her husband, a soldier, died in a skirmish out West somewhere. I forget the details. I offered the only help I could – to bring up her child as my own, as long as she swore never to come here again – though I can see my generosity has been thrown back in my face," he glared down at Edwin, who just looked confused and hurt. Bryony was dumbfounded by his moral code – that he would disown a brother for being so profligate and lascivious, and could feel pity for the women that brother had hurt, yet could not bring himself to offer care to a small boy who was the real victim in all of it.

"So, the boy is not your son Sir, nor yours Ma'am?" Bryony clarified, trying to get to the bottom of the chaos around her. It was not for her to judge the Haverthwaites, but she did need to make sure that Edwin would be cared for when she left.

"But I thought he must be yours, why else would you insist we bring him up as our own?" Mrs Haverthwaite asked, sinking down into a chair, defeated and broken by her husband's lies and half truths. He did not answer her.

"Take him Miss Shaw, and leave this house," Mr Haverthwaite said curtly. "I shall ensure neither of you want for anything." He made no move to comfort his wife, and he did not even glance at the boy as he swept from the room.

"Sir, I will take my wages owed – but not a penny more from you," Bryony called out across the hallway.

"As you will," he retorted.

# Chapter Four

The train was late, and Cody wished there was something he could do to calm the nerves he felt. He had bitten his nails to the quick, and had paced up and down the same stretch of the station platform, that he wouldn't have been surprised to see a groove form beneath his feet. Miss Shaw had said in her last letter that she had a surprise for him, and that she was on her way to Fort Worth to meet with him. He admired her spirit, to give up her position and to travel across the country after such a short correspondence. He had spent many nights worrying if he had done the right thing in inviting her, but he so longed for a partner that he was sure that his impulsive action would never be amongst his many regrets.

Finally the sound of a whistle in the distance, and a plume of smoke billowing into the bright blue sky announced the arrival of the train. It eased into the station, and people began to clamber onboard, whilst others emerged from the carriages. Cody looked up and down the platform for a woman alone, wondering why he had not asked such a simple question as to the color of her hair. But everyone who had stepped down upon the platform seemed to already have been claimed. He wondered if she had maybe fallen asleep. He rushed towards the train, wanting to check the carriages before it pulled out of the station again.

A small boy rushed towards him. Cody smiled at him, but brushed past him. The boy tugged on his pants. "Are you Mr Jenkins?" he asked. Cody stared at him, his brows furrowing.

"I am, now I don't know you do I?" he asked.

"No Sir," the lad said with a grin. "At least you didn't. You do now. Edwin Haverthwaite," he said sticking out his hand. Cody took it and shook it firmly as he was so clearly intended to. The little boy was so solemn, but then the name struck him. Haverthwaite, the name of Miss Shaw's employers. This was the boy who had suffered with influenza.

"You came with Miss Shaw?" he said, wondering what on earth would have possessed Bryony to bring someone else's child with her.

"I did. Turns out my Mama and Papa aren't my parents at all," the boy said with a sniff, as if he was determined not to show just how much this had hurt him. "They don't want me. Bry'ny said she did. So, here I am."

"And where is Miss Shaw?" Cody asked, aghast at how callous this made the Haverthwaites sound. Surely no person would turn a child out of their home, a child they had raised as if he were their own?

"Sorry Mr Jenkins, I was trying to find a porter," a bright and breezy sounding voice said behind him. He spun on his heel. A tall brunette, wearing a smart hat and a faded floral gown stood before him, smiling awkwardly. She had the longest lashes, and the deepest, richest brown eyes. He felt his breath catch. "I told Edwin to stay where he was until I returned, but he is such an inquisitive soul. I wanted to explain this to you properly."

"Oh I think Edwin gave me a pretty thorough appraisal of the situation," Cody joked nervously.

"I couldn't leave him there, unwanted and unloved," she said, putting her hands on Edwin's shoulders in a protective gesture. Cody could see how much she cared for the boy. He hadn't expected this to be the surprise, but it impressed him that she had such a big heart.

"No, I doubt any good Christian could," he agreed.

"You don't mind?" she asked anxiously.

"Not at all. I may have to build a bigger house though," he teased.

"Oh my, I didn't even think of that," Miss Shaw said, raising a hand to her mouth. "I should have told you in my letter. It was all just so sudden."

"Don't fret Miss Shaw, the house is big enough for another three or four Edwin's," he said with a grin. She smiled, and sighed heavily.

"I am so glad you don't mind. I couldn't bear the thought of parting with him now, but I so wanted to meet you too – to see if we might suit."

"Well, we have a few days to do so," Cody said. "Wilbur has agreed to milk the girls for me, as well as his own chores until the end of the week, so we have time."

"Can we go to the park?" Edwin piped up. Cody mussed his hair, the lad ducked away from him playfully.

"We can. There is a mighty fine one right next to the hotel I have booked for you. I just hope they will have a room for you son." Edwin flushed at his use of the word, as if he was happy. Cody's heart went out to the poor, unwanted lad.

"He can share with me if needs must," Bryony said softly. "Thank you, Mr Jenkins. I know this must come as a bit of a shock."

"What is life if not a series of surprises?" Cody chuckled. "Now, let us get you settled at the hotel, and then we can find somewhere to eat."

They walked in silence for a few moments. Miss Shaw looked quite calm and composed, but Cody couldn't seem to stop his mind from wandering back and forth over their meeting. Edwin scampered around them, his curiosity getting the better of him as he looked in shop windows, gaped at the battered old carts and wagons that trundled up and down the Main Street and introduced himself to everyone he met. "He is a lively boy," he remarked.

"Yes, he is. He so desperately wants to be liked though," Miss Shaw said thoughtfully.

"The Haverthwaites didn't do that too well, did they?"

"No, they did not. I used to make excuses for them. Mr Haverthwaite was a member of Congress, and they travelled a lot because of it. But I would never dream of doing so now. Not after the way they treated him. I know wealthy people don't treat children the same way as my family did, that leaving them in the care of a Nanny, and sending them off to school is quite normal – but it isn't right. Children need love, and affection to grow and bloom."

"I was one of those boys, sent away to school," Cody said. Miss Shaw blushed.

"I did not mean to cause any offense," she said quickly.

"None taken, I would never wish to put a child through it myself. It is hard to be a young boy and think that your parents do not want you. But, I got myself expelled every time. My parents gave up in the end and I was schooled at home – but I still didn't see that much of either of them. My Father still wonders why I did not wish to follow in his footsteps. He believed that my lack of formal education would mean he could control my life forever, but it wasn't a life I wished to stay in."

"It must have been very difficult," Miss Shaw said honestly. "To make the choices you did. But, I bet you were a tearaway – just like Edwin. But I truly believe that if he had ever had the love he so craves he would not be so difficult."

"You are probably right. I am sure I would have been a better, happier child if my parents had ever once looked upon me with kindly, rather than contemptuous eyes."

"So what kinds of mischief did you have to get into, to get yourself expelled," she said, her eyes crinkling at the edges as she smiled. She had the most adorable dimples, one in the very center of each cheek.

"Frogs in the porridge, spiders in the master's slippers – the usual boyish pranks," he replied. "I'd lay a wager that you were a very good girl."

"And you would lose your bet," she admitted. "I wasn't bad in school, my parents had to work very hard to send me there and I appreciated the opportunity – but I was a terror outside of my lessons. I was always the one in our tenement that came up with the naughtiest games, and I cannot remember many nights as a girl where I wasn't sent to bed without any supper." She giggled. The sound brought happiness to Cody's heart. "But my Mama was kind, and she always smuggled in some bread and cheese to me, so I didn't have to try and get to sleep with an empty belly."

"She sounds wonderful," he said.

"She was, and so was my Papa though he was strict. He gave us rules because he cared. He never once raised a hand to any of us – and that was rare enough where we were – and he always made sure he gave us a cuddle, and dried our tears when we were sad."

Cody stopped outside a large, whitewashed building. "This is the Grand Hotel," he said proudly. "My Grandpa built it."

"It is beautiful. "So does your family still own it?" Miss Shaw asked.

"I wouldn't have brought you here if they did," he said with a wry smile. "No, Papa sold it as soon as Grandpa died. But I love the old place."

"Edwin, come along inside," Miss Shaw said, turning to the boy. He was busy chatting with a street vendor, who had a cart full of roasted nuts that he was busy scooping into little paper bags.

"May I have some," the boy asked. "I am so hungry." As if on cue his stomach growled loudly. They all laughed, and Cody stepped forward and handed over a few coins and picked up a bag of the hot, salty treats for each of them. "Thank you Sir," Edwin said, so grateful for such a tiny gesture that Cody wanted to pull the boy to him and hold him tightly until he realized he was cared for. He looked at Miss Shaw's sad eyes, and knew that she felt the very same way.

# Chapter Five

Bryony sat on the bed, and wondered how an entire week had passed so quickly. She had never had much time for leisure, and it had been a revelation to her to just be able to get up when she wished each morning, to have breakfast brought to her, and to decide on a whim what to do each day. But, she was already beginning to tire of it. She missed being busy, and having a purpose to her days, though of course taking care of Edwin gave her that. Every morning he would burst into her room, to share a cup of chocolate together before they made their way downstairs to the grand dining room to have breakfast with Mr Jenkins. Every morning, she would pin her hair extra carefully, would pinch her cheeks to heighten her color, and would bite at her lips a little to bring more blood to them. Edwin always laughed at her primping, but she so desperately wanted Mr Jenkins to be proud to have her on his arm.

Now, she was packing. Whatever happened today, she would be leaving the Grand Hotel tomorrow. Whether Mr Jenkins wished her to stay, or whether he intended to put her on a train back to Baltimore she did not know – but she prayed every night that he wanted her to travel onward with him to Faith Creek. He was such a kind man, and was such fun. He had been a wonder with Edwin, offering the boy his attention and his generosity at every turn. She couldn't not remember a time in her life when she had laughed more, nor a time when she had felt so truly special. Yet he had not once asked if he could call her by her first name, rather than the terribly formal Miss Shaw, nor had he tried to take her hand or even her arm. She feared that he did not find her attractive, that he was simply waiting for this day to come so he could say goodbye to her politely then go about his business.

The door burst open, and Edwin appeared, a huge grin splitting his cheeks. She had wondered if he would ever find his smile in the weeks that had followed their leaving Baltimore, but it seemed that Texas was good for him too. "Good Morning Bry'ny," he chirped happily. "The weather is fine, again, and Mr Jenkins says he will take us to the botanical gardens today."

"Well that sounds like a wonderful outing. I'll fetch my hat and gloves and we'll go downstairs to meet him shall we?" Edwin nodded at her eagerly. Bryony moved to the hat stand by the window, and picked up the items she needed. She bent down to check her image in the looking glass, and satisfied she pinned her hat into place, stood up as she pulled on her gloves, and took the boy's hand and led him from the room.

She paused only momentarily at the top of the broad staircase, looking down she could see Mr Jenkins standing in the foyer, awaiting their arrival. From the very first she had thought him handsome. He had strong face, with chiseled features, a strong and straight nose, and the brightest green eyes. His hair was brown, but the sun had added golden strands that brightened it up. He was tall, with broad shoulders and slim hips. Any woman would find him attractive, and she had seen many give him a second glance as they passed him in the street. He truly could have any woman he wished for, so why he had felt the need to advertise for a bride, she was unsure.

"We shall be having breakfast elsewhere today," he announced as Edwin bounded up to him and they shook hands solemnly. She looked at him quizzically.

"We shall?"

"Indeed. An old friend of mine is opening her bakery today, Wilbur's daughter in fact. I promised the old coot I would go along to support her, and to make sure she sold at least a loaf of bread and some pastries. She is the most incredible cook, you will not find one better anywhere in Texas."

"Indeed," she said, giving him a disapproving look. He blanched. "I'm sorry, I didn't…"

"Don't be," she chuckled, glad her little ruse had caught him out. "I am a good cook, but I am not good enough to open my own bakery."

"I shall be the judge of that, someday soon," he said casually. Bryony felt her heart lift, it meant that he did not want her to go home at least. She would not let herself get too hopeful though, he may not have even thought about it, and his offhand comment might mean nothing.

"I think we should go," she said, trying to keep hold of her surging emotions. "I know Edwin can be especially cranky when he doesn't have his breakfast."

"Me too," Mr Jenkins said, turning to the boy and grinning at him. "I shall lead the way."

He took them on a winding tour of the streets of Fort Worth. They hurried past the Army barracks, and Edwin watched as a small corps of men marched past, their uniforms neatly pressed with every button gleaming in the sunlight. The boy shouldered an imaginary musket, and began to march a few steps ahead of them. Bryony smiled. It was incredible to see him so happy, and so settled. Yet, nothing was certain, and she feared that she might let him down again, and cause him upheaval he did not need. She glanced at Mr Jenkins' profile, he was smiling proudly down on Edwin. He turned to her, and she swiftly looked away. She did not want him to see how desperately she wanted him to want her, and she knew it had been written all over her face.

Around the next bend a large crowd was gathered around a little shop. The sign said 'Eleanor's Pastry Shop'. It was painted in bright greens and yellows, and Bryony had never seen such a beautiful display of baked goods anywhere. Loaves of bread that looked like sheaves of wheat, and ears of corn, cakes decorated with tiny frosted rose petals, and pies and pasties of all shapes and sizes. She could feel her mouth salivating, just looking at them. The scent seemed to envelope the entire street, it was so rich and enticing. Mr Jenkin's elbowed his way through the crowds, grabbing her wrist, as she held tightly to Edwin's hand. His touch made her shiver with anticipation; his hand was warm, the callused skin rubbing against hers made her feel almost giddy.

"Cody! Whatever are you doing here?" the pretty blonde behind the counter cried when she spotted him. She rushed out and hugged him. Bryony felt a pang of envy that almost ripped her in two. Mr Jenkins gazed at the petite woman in his arms, his eyes full of love.

"Your father told me I was not to miss your opening day, and to take him back three of your steak pies, two of your finest loaves, and – as he put it – 'some of those fancy french thingummy's'. So, you know he is quite well and just as incorrigible as ever Eleanor." They laughed together, clearly their friendship was close. Byrony wanted to melt back into the crowd, so she didn't have to see just how besotted Mr Jenkins was with his Eleanor.

"I shall pack them up and more. I know he doesn't take care of himself – and he told me that you now have an ice room?" Eleanor said,

"You need it in Texas when you run a dairy. It is quite a sight when those huge blocks of ice are delivered I can tell you," he gushed. "But, that is not important. I have two hungry people with me, who have not had their breakfast because I told them that you bake the best food in all Texas. So don't you let me down, or poor Miss Shaw, and Edwin here are going to go hungry." He turned, and pulled Bryony forwards. Shyly she shook hands with Eleanor.

"I can recommend the strawberry tarts for you young man," Eleanor said to Edwin, "and I think one of the French pastries for you Miss Shaw." Bryony watched as she bustled efficiently behind the counter. Eleanor presented them with a mock bow. "Let me know what you think."

Bryony bit cautiously into the unusual looking pastry. It was so light, and it flaked away and melted in her mouth. She had never tasted anything so rich and buttery and yet so delicate. "Oh, I am sorry," she said as she realized how many crumbs were falling.

"Don't be, I like to see people enjoy their food," Eleanor said. "Now, I know I will be able to tempt you with a chicken and leek pie to take back with you Cody, but what takes your fancy for your breakfast?" Bryony watched as he pointed towards a thick slab of chocolate cake, with a cheeky grin on his face. "For breakfast?" Eleanor said aghast.

"I am only here today, tomorrow we set off for Faith Creek. I have to get my pleasures while I can," he wheedled, but he didn't need to convince her. Eleanor was already cutting him a large slice. He ate it with gusto, as eager as Edwin had been with his tart. When he finished his mouth was rimmed with the thick frosting, and he even had a tiny fleck on the tip of his nose. Bryony watched jealously as Eleanor reached over the counter with a handkerchief, and wiped it off tenderly.

"You, get your hands of my wife," a big bear of a man said as he bustled into the shop from the bakery behind, carrying a tray full of freshly baked loaves. He set them down, and clasped Cody in a hug. "You had your chance, and you blew it." They laughed. Bryony felt all at sea, there were undercurrents here she did not understand.

"Henry, you are a lucky man and I am more than glad to see that even on your first day this enterprise looks like it will be a definite success," Mr Jenkins said, slapping Henry on the arm affectionately. "But, now I shall pay for all out fairings, and then we shall be on our way. We have much to do today," he said, giving Edwin a big wink. The boy nodded excitedly.

"We are to go to the botanical gardens," he said.

"They are very fine, and I am sure you will enjoy them," Eleanor said, beckoning him to come towards the counter. She handed him a chunk of brittle he had been eyeing, and patted him on the head. "Have a wonderful day, and I am sorry we did not have time to get better acquainted Miss Shaw. I do hope that Cody will bring you to supper with us soon."

"You get your shop up and running, and then come and see us. Your Papa would be glad to see you and his grandbaby," Mr Jenkins said with a grin, hugging both Eleanor and Henry tightly. He ushered Bryony and Edwin back through the crowds and into the street.

The further they were away from the little shop, the more Bryony began to think she had imagined the definite chemistry between Mr Jenkins and Eleanor. After all, the woman's husband hadn't seemed worried by it. She tried to make her voice light and bright as they made their way to the gardens. Once inside, she wandered slowly, looking at every label and every plant in minute detail as Mr Jenkins and Edwin rushed around her, playing games and enjoying the fine weather. They reached an elegant water feature, and Bryony stopped to take a seat on the ornate wrought iron bench beside it. Mr Jenkins came and sat by her side, while Edwin capered on the grass, chasing the birds.

"Are you alright my dear?" he asked her softly. She looked at her feet, not sure if she was able to confess to her jealousy of that woman, her fear that he would send her away.

"I am quite well," she assured him, but her voice quavered.

"You have been very quiet today. Ever since we were at Eleanor's."

"It was warm in there, and I felt a little overwhelmed," she admitted. He took her chin in his hand and turned her face so she was looking in his eyes. She tried to pull away. He had so rarely touched her, and to be so close to him already had her heart beating so fast and so hard she feared it might burst its confines and leap right out of her chest.

"Are you sure that is all?" he said holding her face firmly, but tenderly. "When I think on it, you were a little unsettled when we said goodnight, last evening, and this morning too."

She pushed his hands away roughly, and moved further along the bench away from him. Why could he not talk of it either? Why was he making her press him? It did not seem very gallant. "What is to become of us?" she finally asked baldly.

"Ahh!" he said. "You fear I intend to pack you onto a train

tomorrow – or is it that you fear I won't? You are terribly difficult to read. I simply don't know what you want me to say."

"I am difficult to read? She exploded, staring at his eyes, dancing with merriment. "You have not given me an ounce of encouragement that you like me, have not once called me Bryony – yet you hug and kiss a married woman in front of everyone in Fort Worth." He just kept grinning. Bryony wanted to slap him. Instead she stood up and walked further away from the patch of grass that Edwin was playing on. She did not want him to overhear another rejection. He walked slowly up behind her, and placed a hand on her waist. But he did not turn her to face him, and she was glad of it as she was struggling to contain her emotions.

"Dear Bryony, if that is indeed what you wish me to call you, I did not want to push you into a corner. I wanted you to make up your mind about me, before I insisted upon my own deeds and wants. I have made that mistake before – pushed too hard and ended up pushing the woman I loved away for good."

"Eleanor?" she queried.

"Yes Eleanor. We were childhood sweethearts. I assumed that because we had never been apart that she would want marriage and children. I pressured her into it, not ever noticing that for months she had been pulling away from me as she learned that what she wanted was not the love of a brother – but that of a lover. She simply did not feel that way about me after all that time, after everything we had known together."

"So you are still in love with her?" Bryony said, tears beginning to prick at the back of her eyes. She had known it to be true from the very first moment, he did not love her. He loved Eleanor. No wonder she had felt that surge of envy flood over her in the tiny shop. She had lost him, before she ever even knew he existed. Yet, she loved him still. She felt as if her heart might break.

"Not in the way that you mean," he said, but Bryony was still mired in her own pit of despair. He grabbed her and turned her to face him. "Henry was my friend, he had been away at school He came back, and he was new and exciting. I think Eleanor and I realized that we simply didn't want the same kind of life. I never stopped loving either of them, and never will – though at the time I could have killed Henry for stealing her from me. But, I did not want that to happen again. I did not want to lose someone because we had grown apart and wanted different things. I wanted you to be sure you wanted the life I can offer you – because I simply cannot be anyone else now." He paused and she felt the intensity of his gaze, burning into her very soul. "I fell in love with you from the very first letter you sent to me. I had intended to tell you that long ago, but you seemed to be so indifferent to me – and Edwin being here was such a shock."

"You mean you are not sure if you want a bride that comes with a child?" she asked, turning to face him. She would take any manner of insult to herself, but Edwin had done nothing wrong. He simply wanted to be loved.

"I will admit it wasn't what I expected. I came to the station to meet a woman – and was presented with a ten year old boy too. But, that is not the reason I held back. You just didn't seem to like me very much," he said. "Did I get it so wrong?" She looked down at her feet, not knowing how to respond.

"Yes," she whispered. "Yes, you got it so very wrong. I fell in love with you the moment I read your advertisement. I used to laugh at the people who wrote those things. I couldn't imagine ever wanting to find a husband by mail order. But I found you. And then when I got off the train and you hid your surprise so well, in front of Edwin and myself at least, about my arriving with him. I couldn't help but love you more. But you never spoke of your intentions – you never even stopped to ask if I wanted to be called Miss Shaw."

"You never asked if I would prefer Cody either," he countered with a grin, taking her face between his palms. He bent his lips to hers and kissed her tenderly. "I do, by the way." She smiled, as the tears fell down her cheeks. He wiped them tenderly away with his thumb, and pressed kisses on her forehead, her eyes, her cheeks and the tip of her nose before claiming her lips once more. "Will you marry me Bryony, and come back to Faith Creek with me where I intend to look into formally adopting Edwin and making him my son."

Bryony bit her lip, and stared at him, then at Edwin. She tried to speak, but her words caught in her throat as she sobbed. "Oh, I will," she finally managed to utter. "I will."

# Epilogue

Henry ran up the aisle of the tiny chapel towards Cody. "So sorry, got held up by the little one. Melissa is teething, and she was so crotchety on the drive here. She hated every bump of the wagon on that rutted track."

"You made it my friend, that is all I could ever ask of you." Cody welcomed the embrace of his old friend, and felt his nerves steady just having his reassuring hulk stood beside him.

"I left Melly with Wilbur. He's on his way down any second and Eleanor is at the boarding house with Bryony," Henry said. Cody took a deep breath, at least the people he loved the most would all be here to see them wed. Bryony had no family, and he didn't care if his mother and father came, but it would be nice if his siblings came with their families. He had sent the invitations, but he doubted any of them would make the journey. As long as Bryony came, and Edwin was there to escort her down the aisle then everything would be just fine.

"Are you ready for this?" the minister asked him. He'd come from Amarillo, especially to marry them and he looked a little tired from the

*Mail Order Bride - Bryony's Destiny*

journey. But Cody was glad he had made the effort for them.

"I was ready over a month ago," he admitted. "But we had to do things right." Henry grinned at him.

"Tell the truth, you were ready years ago – you just got the wrong girl first time around." Cody laughed.

"I cannot deny it. All I have ever wanted is a wife and family of my own – probably because I wasn't welcome in my own family growing up." He watched as Wilbur wandered towards them, Melissa was dressed in lace, and even from a distance Cody could see that the child was covered in crumbs. "I take it you brought some custard tarts with you?" he said to Henry who turned to see his father-in-law take his seat.

"The old coot couldn't even wait until after the ceremony," he whistled.

"Eleanor is just too good," Cody said as they watched her rush up the aisle and take her baby from her father. Henry blew his wife a kiss, and Cody winked at her. She smiled back at them, and nodded knowingly.

A lone violin began to play the wedding march, the chapel was too small to hold an organ or even a pianoforte. But Cody rather liked the sound of it, it made the tune somehow more cheerful, lighter. A figure dressed all in white walked towards him. By her side Edwin beamed with pride. When they reached the altar, Edwin handed Bryony's hand to Cody. Cody took it, but then moved to embrace the lad. He blushed pink, but looked pleased as punch as he took his seat.

Bryony pushed back her veil, and Cody couldn't help but lean forward to kiss her, she looked so beautiful. "Too early," she whispered cheekily.

The rest of the ceremony passed in a blur, as Cody remained lost in his bride's big brown eyes. Every time her lashes swept down over her cheek he wanted her to look up, when she looked up at him her gaze was so full of love he felt undeserving and wished she would lower her eyelids once more. But when he heard the final words the minister spoke, he could have crowed with happiness.

"I now pronounce you husband and wife. You, Sir, may kiss your bride," the kindly man said.

"See this was where you were supposed to …" Cody cut Bryony off, pulling her towards him and kissing her as if nobody was watching. He had never felt so alive, so happy in all his life. They walked down the aisle, and he noticed, right at the back of the chapel, that his entire family was stood, waiting for him.

"Congratulations son," his father said warmly. His mother embraced him and his siblings crowded around him offering their best wishes. For the first time in his life he felt truly accepted by them all, and he vowed to ensure that Edwin would feel this way every single day of his life.

"Mother, Father, I would like to introduce you to my wife, gosh that sounds good to say! This is Bryony, and our son Edwin," he said pulling the boy forward proudly.

"But I'm not your son," he said innocently. "I'm not anybody's son anymore."

"Oh yes you are sweetheart," Bryony said with a smile as Cody pulled a sheet of paper from his pocket. "According to the law, you are very much our son – if you want to be?" She took the document from Cody and handed it to the boy. He read it slowly, his lips moving as he spelled out the words.

"You adopted me?" he said. "What does that mean exactly?"

"It means that according to the law you are our son. But, this is just a piece of paper. More importantly you are our son because we both love you very much," Cody explained.

"So I can call you Mama?" he asked Bryony. She nodded. "And you Papa."

"If you want to," Bryony said. "If you don't then that is your choice. But this piece of paper assures you that we will always look after you – whatever you choose to call us."

"I get to choose my parents? Wow! Because if I could, I would always have chosen you Bry'ny – sorry Mama," Edwin said burying himself in her body and flinging his arms around her tightly. When he emerged, Cody could see the tracks where his tears had fallen. "Papa, I like that. I like that you are my Papa."

"I like that you like it," said Cody as he put an arm round his wife, and the other around his son.

The End

Thank you for reading and supporting my book and I hope you enjoyed it.

Please will you do me a favor and leave a review so I'll know whether you liked it or not, it would be very much appreciated, thank you.

# Other books by Karla

Sun River Brides Series
Ruby Springs Brides Series
Silver River Brides Series
Eagle Creek Brides

# About Karla Gracey

Karla Gracey was born with a very creative imagination and a love for creating stories that will inspire and warm people's hearts. She has always been attracted to historical romance including mail order bride stories with strong willed women. Her characters are easy to relate to and you feel as if you know them personally. Whether you enjoy action, adventure, romance, mystery, suspense or drama- she makes sure there is something for everyone in her historical romance stories!

CPSIA information can be obtained
at www.ICGtesting.com
Printed in the USA
LVHW092040280321
682767LV00024B/573

9 781542 300018